His House

A Parable of Spiritual Intimacy

Judy Boozer

ISBN: 978-1-954808-00-3

First printing, 2018.

Publisher: Judy Boozer

Arise, my darling, my beautiful one, come with me. See! The winter is past; the rains are over and gone. Flowers appear on the earth; the season of singing has come; the cooing of doves is heard in our land. The fig tree forms its early fruit; the blossoming vines spread their fragrance. Arise, come, my darling; my beautiful one, come with me.

Song of Songs 2:10-13

Table of Contents

To the Lover -

Beloved,
My sky is on fire
And You
Have set it ablaze

The Sign

As I walked along the path, I came upon a group gathered around the base of what appeared to be a sign. The sign was flashing neon with a gyrating arrow pointing down a path. The flashing neon words said, "This way to God's house." The people milling about seemed enthralled with the sign, often pointing to it and exclaiming its wonders.

I asked one of the passersby about the sign. He told me what I already knew; the sign pointed to the path that led to God's house. Excitedly he told me how grateful he was to have it, after such a long journey through the desert. He hurried to join the group gathered around the base of the sign. They appeared to be setting up a potluck and eagerly greeted one another. I joined them.

During dinner, individuals easily shared their experience of the sign: when they saw it, how it made them feel, the comfort it gave them to see it flashing in the night. Curious, I asked if any of them had traveled down the path the sign pointed to. They looked at me in shock, as if I had suggested something impossible.

"Of course not!" they said, "It's not safe. That path leads to the Valley of the Shadow of Death. Death, as in dead, as in no longer living. Almost no one who goes down that path returns and those who do speak in riddles. We can only assume that path leads to madness and death. Besides, we know where God is. The sign tells us where He is. That path is for after we die. As long as we're here, we can show other people where God is. Isn't that the Great Commission?"

As I lay down for the night, I couldn't help but wonder why someone would build a sign pointing to a path no one is supposed to take. The next day I told my new friends that I was traveling down the path to God's house. They tried to dissuade me, reminding me that it was unsafe and expressing their concerns for me. I told them that I had to know the purpose of the sign. I should not have been concerned for as soon as I left their sight they returned to adoring the sign.

The journey through the Valley of the Shadow of Death was challenging, more challenging than I could have anticipated. There were twists and turns, false paths, hidden paths, and the darkness that permeated my soul. When I called out, my voice echoed back different and yet somehow the same, mocking me. There were times when I thought I would die there and there were other times I thought I already had.

Suddenly, and almost without warning, I stumbled upon His door. I couldn't believe I hadn't seen it sooner. The porch light shone in the darkness like a lighthouse and yet I had been blind to it. Seeing it was like opening my eyes: before I walked in the dark because my eyes were closed and now I walked in the light because my eyes were open. I knocked. He answered.

He seemed different than what I expected. I expected hell and brimstone, He was more like "come in and have dinner with me." I looked around as if expecting to see that His home had been hard to find. It was not. If I looked carefully through the trees, I could even see the group gathered around the base of the sign, singing songs and holding hands.

I looked at him. He looked at me. I said, "Did you know that there is a group of people at the corner gathered around a sign pointing to your house?"

"Yes," He said. "Some of my oldest friends built that sign so that others would have an easier time finding my home. There are others elsewhere. However, many confuse knowing where I am for knowing who I am, and so they gather around the sign instead of coming to visit me."

"What about the forest, the Valley of the Shadow of Death? It seemed so much bigger when I was walking through it. However, now that I'm here, it seems so small. What happened to it?"

"The Valley of the Shadow of Death is the journey of dying to self. It always seems bigger, harder, and scarier when you're walking through it than it does when you're finished. That's because you see it through the eyes of your flesh when you're walking through it and your false self is afraid to die. However, when your false self is dead, you see it through the eyes of your true self, which cannot die, and you are not afraid. The false self keeps many from making this journey."

"The people said that most who make this journey never return and those who do return speak in riddles. Has no one returned to tell them what to expect on this journey so that they're not afraid?"

"Many have returned. However, they have not returned the same as when they left. Some are not recognized. Those who are recognized speak a different language, a language that sounds like nonsense because it speaks of a deeper truth instead of surface facts. This journey cannot be taught; it is not information or data. It can only be experienced firsthand. The sign is intended to point toward the journey, not to be a substitute for that journey. Still, those who have found the sign have gotten closer than if there had been no sign. It still serves a purpose."

He smiled at me like an old friend and stepped back, inviting me in. "I'm glad you came. I was just about to sit down to dinner. Please join me." And so, I did.

The Hall of Mirrors

"It's time," He said, looking at me.

"Time for what?" I asked.

"Time to revisit the Valley of the Shadow of Death."

"I thought we were finished with that. Haven't we already conquered that? I walked through it to get here."

"The Valley is always there, growing and expanding. I planned, planted, and shaped the Valley. There will come a time when you recognize the Valley as your friend, not your enemy. There may even be a day when you ask Me to take you through the Valley instead of waiting for it like a punishment."

"What should I bring?"

"You can bring whatever you want. Just know that whatever you bring will be left behind there."

As we approached the Valley of the Shadow of Death, I was surprised. It didn't look like a valley at all. It looked like a big circus tent. I looked around confused.

"Where are the trees?" I asked. "Where is the forest? This is not how it looked when I last walked through."

"The Valley of the Shadow of Death changes as you do. Before, you saw it through eyes filled with fear, so it was frightening, and you were lost. Today you're not afraid, so you see it in a different form."

I heard the carnival pipe organ playing and saw the lights flashing. Above the entrance to the tent, I saw the sign that said Hall of Mirrors. I thought that this might not be so bad. After all, mirrors can't really hurt you.

He took me to a tall mirror with an ornate frame made of gold. Within the frame were a million masks reflecting various emotions. It was like looking at a kaleidoscope of humanity. The mirror was set at a slight angle toward the ceiling, so I had to step in front of the mirror to see myself. I laughed out loud at my reflection. My head was huge, my waist was small, and my feet were huge. I looked like a clown.

He smiled and said, "So you see, this is an illusion." I nodded, still laughing at my reflection. Did He think I could be fooled by something so obvious?

He took me to another mirror. This one was small and rectangular, set at eye level. The frame was silver polished so that it practically glowed. When I saw my face, I gasped softly with delight. My face looked angelic: soft, gentle, and kind. My eyes looked out with unending patience. The silver frame looked like a halo. I stared at my face in admiration. Then He waved His hand, and the image disappeared. I looked at Himquestioningly, robbed of my prize.

"This also is an illusion," He said. "Look again."

I looked again and instead of the angelic face, I saw a haughty one. My nose lifted in pride. My eyebrows raised in criticism and my eyes looking back at me, full of self-righteousness. The shining silver halo framing my face seemed obscene. My heart broke. I looked away, disgusted, embarrassed, and ashamed.

"Understand that even this is also an illusion," He said as He stepped to my side.

"The Hall of Mirrors is called the Valley of the Shadow of Death because your false selves die here. Here is where you learn to see your true self. Here is where you learn to be your true self. For your false self, this is the Valley of Death. But you are not your false self. For your true self, this is only a shadow of death."

"How then do I become who I wish to be? When I try to become who I want to be, I become the embodiment of what I most hate. How is there hope for me? How can I be saved from myself?"

"The natural way of thinking focuses on the results and hopes the process will figure itself out. I focus on the process knowing that the results are already Mine anyway. To become who you wish to be, stop focusing on who you wish to be and simply live as you are. The challenge is in seeing who you are without judging who you are. That's what the Hall of Mirrors produces: the ability to see things as they are, not as you expect or imagine them to be. You are neither good nor bad. You simply are."

I looked back at the silver frame and saw yet a different face. This one looked at me with questioning eyes, unsure. My face no longer raised with pride, my eyebrows no longer critical.

His face softened into a smile and He said, "There it is...do you see it?" For the first time, I looked without expectation of what I should find, searching for some hidden detail.

"See what?"

"Humility," He said as He put His arm around my shoulder and looked at me through the mirror.

The Dishes

One night, after dinner, we sat at the table and reminisced about the day. I told a story about a bird I had seen that morning with a bright, blue jacket and small, dark eyes. I told how I had watched it bounce around, cocking its head and chirping before flying away. From across the table, He smiled knowingly and nodded.

"I *know* that bird," He said. "He comes by every morning hoping for a handout. I fed him once and now he's decided that we're friends." We laughed together. He got up and began to clear the table. He asked if I would mind washing the dishes with him. Of course, I didn't mind.

As I carried the serving plate into the kitchen, He squirted me from the faucet, laughing. I squealed and put down the plate, chasing Him through the kitchen. We laughed, joked, and sprayed each other from the faucet as we washed the dishes and cleaned up the kitchen. As far as I know, I won...as long as winning is determined by who is the wettest. I loved it.

The next night, after dinner, we sat and chatted about the day. After a few minutes, I began to clear the table. I moved to the kitchen. He stayed at the table. I began to wash the dishes, truthfully hoping He would follow...hoping for a repeat of the night before, but He stayed at the table drinking His coffee, quietly contemplating, alone in His thoughts. I refilled His cup twice before I was finished with the dishes. I felt disappointed and reminded myself that I couldn't, shouldn't expect Him to entertain me. After all, it was His house.

The third night, after dinner was over, I immediately began cleaning the table. I wordlessly took the dishes into the kitchen, ran the water, put away the food, and began to wash the dishes. As I was drying the copper stew pot, He came into the kitchen.

"What are you doing?" He said.

Startled, I looked up thinking that what I was doing must be obvious. I looked around at the dishes and the water and then at Him.

"I'm cleaning up," I said. "Y'know, washing the dishes."

"Why?"

"I don't know; I guess it needs to be done."

His eyebrows came together and His lips turned into a straight line. "Do you think I invited you here to do chores for me?" I opened my mouth to answer even as no words came. The truth was that I knew what I was supposed to say, but it wasn't what I wanted to say.

"Well, it's just that the first night we had so much fun. I loved that. I wanted to do that every night, but the second night you stayed at the table and I did it alone. You didn't stop me. I thought that you wanted me to do the dishes from now on. I guess it's not unreasonable. I have been staying at your house for a while now. I mean, it can't be fun and games forever, right? You made dinner so it's fair that I clean up. I know how these things work."

"You don't have to earn your keep here. You are my cherished guest and it is my joy to serve you. You are my friend and I enjoy your delight."

His shoulders slumped slightly as if He just realized that He'd lost something. "When I asked you to wash the dishes with me, the most important part of that was 'with me.' If I wished, the dishes would do themselves. I didn't need you to do the dishes. I wanted you to do them *with me*, to enjoy being *with me*, to laugh *with me*, to have fun *with me*, to share your stories *with me*. Last night, I would have been thrilled if you'd sat at the table *with me*, drinking coffee, and left the dishes to themselves."

I stood there stunned with the copper pot hanging from my hand, forgotten. I had missed an opportunity to sit across the table and drink coffee with my friend, my partner, my love and, instead, I had been elbow-deep in soapy water, longing for Him, disappointed in my aloneness. I felt so stupid, absolutely blind. A pregnant silence hung in the air. I didn't know what to say.

He took the pot from my hand and set it in its place. "Would you come sit outside on the porch with Me?"

"I would love to, very much," I said, and we watched the sun set brilliantly with my head resting on His shoulder, a quiet audience to the majesty of living… together.

The Butterfly

I groaned in frustration as I put the book down. It seemed that no matter how hard I tried, I just couldn't get the concepts to move from my head to my heart. It was like I was made of Teflon inside and everything just slid off. I was never going to master them.

Discouraged, I went to find Him. Maybe He could tell me the trick to it all, the secret that would make this easier. He was in the back pantry, with the hallway full of stuff. Unfortunately, it meant I couldn't reach the pantry door, so I just stood in the hallway and shouted to Him. It took a couple of times before His head popped around the corner. He was covered in white powder as if a bag of flour had fallen on Him and exploded.

"Um," I said, not knowing what to say. His face was good-naturedly eager. "Are You ok?"

"Oh, fine." He said. "Just cleaning up a bit. It has to be done ever so often otherwise we'd have bugs and mice. Although they're lovely creatures in their own space, that space is not in My back pantry."

"I'm glad you feel that way," I said, stifling a laugh. I never knew anyone could be that excited about cleaning out a pantry.

"Did you want Me for something?" He asked.

"Um. Yeah. I mean, kind of. It's not that important, I guess." My questions suddenly seemed so insignificant and it was hard to ask them when His head was covered in flour.

"You know," He said, stepping out of the room, "It's time that I took a break. I can finish up after a cup of tea and a cookie or two. Would you like to join Me?"

I smiled, relieved. "I would love to." I put the teapot on to boil and put some cookies on a plate. His favorite tea was His own mixture of cinnamon, cloves, and orange zest. He drank it so often that just smelling it made me feel safe and comfortable. We sat down at the table for an afternoon break.

"How is the book going?" He asked.

I looked down at the table. "Ok, I guess."

He stopped, His cup halfway to His mouth. One eyebrow went up. "Really?" He said.

A disgusted look passed over my face. My shoulders slumped. "No," I confessed.

"Ah." He sipped His tea and reached for a

cookie.

"I just get so frustrated. The concepts seem easy enough to understand, but when I try to put them into practice, it goes kaput. I can't seem to get it together. I can't seem to truly understand them. Maybe there's something wrong with me."

He started to chuckle. "Yes, that must be it. If it's not easy for you, it must be because there's something wrong with you. Tell me, do things usually come easily for you?"

I was a little embarrassed as I considered my answer. The truth is that a lot of things did come easily for me whenever I put my mind to it. I could be quite determined. I realized that I felt frustrated precisely because it wasn't easy and, honestly, I expected it to be. I expected it to be because, deep down, I thought I was pretty awesome, maybe even better than others.

He stood up, walked to the front door, opened it, and walked outside without saying a word. It seemed so odd that I followed Him. He pointed discreetly to the Bee Balm along the front of the house.

"Do you see that?" He whispered. In the field of bright purple flowers, a delicate butterfly sat, its wings rhythmically opening and closing like a breath. I nodded. "Try to catch it," He said. I looked at Him just to confirm I'd heard Him right. He nodded encouragingly. I shrugged my shoulders and stepped toward the plant, my hands cupped and ready to cover the butterfly. However, as soon as I made my final move, it fluttered away. I pursued: running and snatching the air as it flew higher and higher until it was out of my reach. Behind me, He was laughing so hard that He had to sit down. Finally, I returned to where He was sitting. I was hot, tired, and frustrated.

"That was the best thing I ever saw," He laughed. I nodded grimly. "I mean, you were really going after that poor butterfly." I did not appreciate Him making fun of me, so I went back into the house, letting the door slam behind me. I sat back down at the table to finish my tea. I was beginning to think that talking with Him about this was a mistake. He came in after me and sat down in His seat across the table.

"Do you know why the butterfly got away?" He asked.

"Because it can fly?" I said sarcastically.

"Yes, because it can fly...and because you were chasing it," He replied.

"Of course, I was chasing it! You told me to," I said sharply.

"Actually, I told you to catch it. You decided to chase it. Chasing it only made it fly farther out of reach." I wondered when He was going to tell me something I didn't already know.

"To catch a butterfly, you have to not chase it."

"What do you mean?" I asked, still irritated.

"To catch a butterfly, you make it easy for it to catch you," He said, His eyes still laughing. Obviously, I had been unclear in my first question, asking what He meant. I glared at Him from under my eyelashes.

"If you are still and actively wait for the butterfly, it will come to you. Understand, this is not a passive waiting, but an active and intentional waiting. The truth is much the same way. If you try to chase it, it is pushed farther and farther out of your reach. However, when you actively wait, quiet and still, it will catch you." Suddenly, He had my attention.

"What does that mean?" I asked, trying to picture how that looked in real life.

"Meditation and contemplation are two ways to make yourself still inside so that the truth can find you. It's about making the mind and heart still and quiet. If you try to understand truth with only the mind or only the emotions, it will escape you. Truth is for the whole person, not part of a person. When you chased the butterfly, you did it with all you had. However, you can't catch a butterfly when you haven't mastered yourself. How can you understand the truth when you haven't mastered yourself?"

I thought about what He'd said as I finished my tea and cookies. He returned to the back pantry and I returned to my book. This time, however, instead of trying to understand it with my mind, I let myself savor the truth in those words. I let them hang in the air while I considered them. I thought about alternative ways those words might point to different parts of the truth, not just the first way I saw. I challenged myself to catch the butterfly of truth by making myself still enough for it to catch me. The moment a truth caught me is still emblazed in my memory. It was like the sun came up and I finally saw. That was when I knew He was telling me the truth. That was when I started to trust Him in my heart.

Pinocchio

One afternoon, He handed me a large box, wrapped in a beautiful bow.

"A gift? For me? What's the occasion?" I asked.

"Open it," He said, smiling.

I untied the bow and opened the box. Inside was a wooden marionette puppet, painted to look like a boy.

"A...puppet...how...interesting," I said, with questions in my eyes. "I've never seen one of these in real life." I lifted the puppet from the box, holding the control bar in my hands so that its feet danced just above the ground. "Um. I'm not really sure what to do with it, I guess."

He smiled and took the control bar from me, moving the puppet around. He showed me how to move the arms and the legs so that it looked like the puppet was walking. Obviously, an expert on marionette puppets, He showed me how its movements could be made to mimic human movement with careful mastery of the control bar, positioned above the strings. However, when I tried, the strings got tangled together and the puppet just hung awkwardly. He laughed good-naturedly at my attempts and encouraged me, saying that I would get better with practice, before leaving me alone with the puppet.

I practiced the rest of the day: making it walk around the room, making it walk up and down stairs, making it appear to hide behind the curtain. I have to admit, I did get better, but I still wouldn't say I was good so much as not horrible.

The next day, He asked me how it was going. I was honest about my progress and frustrations. I told Him that I would start out well, but the longer I worked with the puppet, the more its arms and legs would get tangled in the strings and, before too long, it would be all bound up and I'd have to stop and untangle it. He thoughtfully listened, nodding His head.

"Bring me the puppet," He said. I went and got it, bringing it to Him, expecting Him to show me some trick to controlling the marionette.

"You can always do what I do," He said.

"What's that? Is there some trick?"

He smiled, took out a large pair of scissors, and cut the strings.

I stood in shock, looking between Him and the now-broken puppet. I dropped to my knees, almost without thinking, cradling the puppet in my hands. "What have You done?" I said. "What did You do?" I looked at Him for answers, not really expecting any, but wanting them anyway.

"You are that puppet," He said. "The more you try to pretend to live through religious rules and rituals, the more you get tangled; the more bound up you become. I don't want a puppet, something that I can control. I want the real you. I want to cut your strings and set you free, not control you like a toy. I don't want a control bar; I want your heart. I don't want you to mimic life; I want you to be alive."

I held the puppet in my hands, the strings trailing onto the ground. Honestly, I felt a little angry because I had practiced with that puppet all day long and now, it was for nothing. I couldn't even show off what little I'd learned.

"I don't feel like a puppet. Admittedly, the rules and rituals can be frustrating, but they don't rule my life," I said firmly.

"Don't they?" He asked, lifting one eyebrow slightly. "You're upset over a ruined puppet because you spent time on that puppet and now you don't have anything to show for it. All yesterday, you worked with that puppet. Why?"

"Well, you'd given it to me and I wanted to master it. I wanted to show You that I had mastered it."

"So, you expected a result, a payoff, a reward of some kind?"

"I guess. I expected that You would be impressed and maybe proud of me."

"I'm already impressed and proud of you because I love you. Why did you really work with that puppet?"

I thought for a moment before realization spread in my heart like the sun coming up.

"I worked with that puppet because You gave it to me and I thought I was supposed to master it, that You wanted me to master it." My voice was barely a whisper. "I did it because I thought I was supposed to." He looked at me, saying nothing with His mouth and everything with His face.

"Oh, dear God…I am that puppet. Cut my strings and set me free. I want to be a real person and not a puppet, acting in response to what I think others want from me."

He smiled as He took the broken puppet from my hands and put it on the mantle. "I already have.

You're the one who keeps tying strings around your arms and legs. Pinocchio was a puppet who wanted to be a real person. You've been a real person trying to be a puppet. Let go of being a puppet. It's time to learn to live as the real person you are. We'll do it together."

The Garden

For all of my time with Him, He was still such a mystery to me.

"Have you ever been in love?" I asked Him one day as I folded laundry.

"Why do you ask?" He responded, putting down His pencil and looking up from the letter He was writing.

"I don't know. I'm just curious. I like to think that I know what that's like, but I wanted to know what You thought." I tried to be casual, but I felt like He could see through me. I think I folded the same towel three times before finally putting it away.

He looked at me thoughtfully for a few minutes before picking His pencil back up. "I'm going to take you somewhere special tomorrow," He announced, as if that answered my question, and then continued writing His letter.

The next morning, He led me out of the house and down a path I had never seen before. It wound around a small hill to a wooden gate, set crookedly in a wooden fence. It creaked as He opened it for me.

I looked around in wonder. In every direction, I was surrounded by color. It was His flower garden. I had no idea it was even here. Such brilliance wrapped around me; I felt like I was in a rainbow cocoon, waking from a dream to discover I was a butterfly.

He moved to one of the rows and I followed. It was full of roses; I could smell them before I even got a chance to see them. The scent was intoxicating. I felt like I'd died and gone to rose heaven. Suddenly, I understood why the dog would randomly roll around on the ground, rubbing himself with the scent of grass. Admittedly, I've never wanted to smell like grass, but I would roll around in the rose bushes, minus the thorns of course, if I thought I could smell like this.

He stopped in front of a bush covered in scarlet roses. The color was so saturated that they seemed almost otherworldly. They looked like they were made of velvet. He bent down and pressed His nose into one of the blooms, inhaling deeply. He stood and lifted the flower for me to see.

"What do you think of this one?" He asked.

"It's beautiful. I mean, it's gorgeous," I was

secretly wondering if I could take some of the flowers back to the house...maybe even that one.

"How would you describe it to someone who had never encountered a rose? How would you describe the color to someone who had been born blind? How would you describe the smell to someone who had no sense of smell?" He asked.

I paused for a moment. Every thought I had led me back to the same dead end. Finally, I admitted defeat. "I don't know. How would you describe it to someone who couldn't see or smell?"

"You can't. Anything that you use to describe it would be inadequate. Your best efforts would be inaccurate and misleading. This rose can't be described. It must be experienced. You can't tell someone how it smells; they must smell it. You can't tell someone about the color; they must see it. You can't describe the softness of the petals, they have to feel them."

I had to admit that He was right. Even my best words wouldn't be good enough to describe the beauty of that one flower.

"Love is like that," He said. "It can't be described. It must be experienced. Those who are foolish enough to try to describe it have never experienced it and those who experience it know better than to try to describe it. Once you've experienced it, your focus changes from explaining it so that others don't have to take that path, to doing all that you can to help encourage people to take that path for themselves. All you can do is point the way to where it can be found. Words are not enough. Pictures are not enough. You can only know how the rose smells by smelling it. You can only know how deep the scarlet is by seeing it. You can only know how soft the petals are by rubbing them between your fingers."

"But how will I know if I've experienced love if I don't know what it's like?"

"You don't need to know that the name of this flower is 'rose' to know that its scent is intoxicating. You don't need to understand what type of flower it is to know that the color is rich and deep. You don't need to know that love is called 'love' to know that you were made for it and it was made for you. When we leave this garden, you will carry with you the perfume placed in these flowers. It will cling to you, not because you did anything, but because you were here. When someone has truly experienced love, they carry it into their world, not because they try to, but because it has changed them. They have become the love they experienced."

He took out a small set of clippers and clipped the bloom, handing it to me.

"You asked if I had ever been in love. It's the wrong question, my dear. Truthfully, I **AM** Love, so the better question is whether **you** have ever been in Love, whether your time with Me has changed you. Those who have been in Me and choose to continue to rest there, are always in Love." He smiled and put His hand on my shoulder. "That's a question only you can answer."

The War

One morning, I was wakened by the loud sound of arguing and clanging. I stumbled out of bed and ran to the front room to find Him there, looking out of the picture window.

"Wh-what's going on?!" I asked, wildly looking around, my hair a cloud of confusion around my head.

"They've come to blows," He said, nodding outside.

"Who? What?! Where?"

He turned to me and stifled a laugh. "It can wait until you put a robe on, I think." I realized I was standing in the living room in my pajamas with part of my hair sticking in the air and the other part plastered to my head. I wrapped my arms around myself and smiled weakly.

"And maybe run a brush through my hair," I said to myself as I returned to my room. After putting on my bathrobe, slipping my slippers on, and smoothing my hair down, I came to the front room to find Him brewing a pot of coffee and putting breakfast on the table.

"Is this better?" I said, smiling.

"Well, the other was more interesting, but I didn't think you'd be comfortable that way." The arguing and clanging outside had died down but we could still hear an occasional angry shout.

"What's going on outside?" I asked as I reached for toast and marmalade.

"Do you remember the sign you passed on your way in?"

"Mmhmmm." I nodded with my mouth full.

"Well, another group from a different sign location was on a pilgrimage and they ran into each other."

"I see. And that was a problem?"

"Apparently. They started arguing over which sign was best. It would seem that conversation was heated."

"But don't the signs point to the same place?"

"Oh yes," He said. "I've learned never to underestimate someone's need to be right and, more importantly, make others wrong. In such cases, the truth is the first casualty."

At that moment a loud boom sounded,

shaking the windows. It startled me, and I jumped. However, when I turned to look at him, He didn't even flinch.

"How can you be so calm? Are they trying to blow each other up?!"

"Probably," He said, reaching for another biscuit.

"Are we going to do anything?"

"What do you think we should do?"

"I don't know...something."

"What do you think would work?"

I sat in silence, thinking about that question. What would work? I realized that I had no idea. Throughout the day the conflict escalated. I could hear shouting back and forth punctuated with clanging and the occasional boom. Around mid-afternoon, a silence settled in. After a few minutes, I figured they had worked out their differences and went about my business.

We had dinner in an eerie silence. It was like everything was holding its breath. There weren't even crickets chirping. It was ominous.

I had just gone to bed and was almost asleep when a loud shout erupted from outside. I almost fell out of my bed. I crouched on the floor for a few seconds before realizing where I was. I flew out of my bedroom, colliding with Him in the hallway. I was alarmed. He was not.

"What is it now?!"

"It's war."

"What? What in the world does that mean?" I must admit, I was sharp with him. I generally don't like being shocked from bed, so perhaps I can be forgiven for being a little grumpy.

He took me to the front window and pointed through the forest of the Valley of the Shadow of Death to the corner where the sign stood. I could see flames in the distance. I could see the silhouette of people fighting. I could hear weapons clanging. I could hear battle cries and beyond that the sound of people crying out in pain. I turned to Him with concern on my face.

"How can we help? People are being injured in this war."

His expression told me that I was missing something. I looked again.

"Do you see where the battle is?" He asked. I nodded. "Do you see where it's not?" He continued.

"Well, I see that it seems to be around the sign, but it's not in Your yard," I said. He turned to me and smiled.

"True. To get to My yard, they would have to go through the Valley of the Shadow of Death. They would have to die to themselves. Of course, once they died to themselves, they would have no reason to fight anymore, no need to be right anymore. Notice how they have taken great care to move the battle away from that which requires the death of ego. As long as they choose to fight each other, they will never come to this house. Do you remember when I told you that the false self keeps many from making the journey? This is part of what I meant. If we rush to help the wounded, we would still have to bring that through the Valley and many simply will not come."

"It seems silly to think that all of this is a fight over the location of the sign."

"Actually, this fight started because one sign is made of wood and one sign uses electricity. The group with the wooden sign believed that their sign was the true sign because it was older. The group with the electronic sign felt that their sign appealed to more people, so it was better."

"So, all of this pain and suffering, not to mention confusion, is about the validity of a sign that neither group has actually followed?"

"Such is the way of the false self. It creates confusion to protect itself. It creates fear to protect itself. It creates anger to protect itself. It creates self-righteousness to protect itself. Now do you understand why the Valley of the Shadow of Death is your friend and not your enemy?"

For the first time, with the night on fire and people dying in the distance, I understood.

The Unforgiven

After the night that war was declared, things began to settle down. Two days later, I asked Him if He thought it was safe for me to go see the damage. He assured me that I would be safe, so I grabbed my sweater and my medicine bag and walked through the woods to the corner, where the sign used to stand. There was no happy, singing group there any longer. The sign with the gyrating arrow pointing to the path to God's house was nothing more than a half-burnt stub of a post sticking up from the ground. All around could be heard the quiet moaning of hurt people.

Behind the stubby-sign-stick was a group of three people, sitting on the ground, huddled together. I went to them. As I neared them, I could see the burns on their hands and arms and dried blood around the tears in their clothes. Their faces, however, were covered as they clung to each other for both warmth and comfort.

"Are you alright?" I asked, moving to them.

"Who-What-Who's that?" one said as they bunched together.

I saw the burns on his face as he tried to look around. His eyes were raw and damaged. I realized that he couldn't see.

I knelt in front of him and put my hand on his shoe, which seemed to be the only part of him that wasn't visibly hurt. I said gently, "I am from His house. I travelled through this area not too long ago. Perhaps you remember me."

"No one travels to His house!" the man spat. "You're obviously lying. You're one of them, aren't you? Have you come back to finish the job?!"

"I'm not sure what you mean. I truly am from His house. He sent me with medicine and authorized me to care for the wounded in His name."

"Likely story," One of the man's companions said, lifting her face in my direction. I could see that she also had burns that had damaged her eyes. "We won't be taken advantage of again. You can tell your superiors that."

"Don't you want me to try to help you? I have medicine here that will heal your wounds."

"Heal our wounds?! Absolutely not! We want those followers of a false gospel to see what they've done to us. They should see how they've wounded the disciples of the true God." The third companion shouted the last part out in a random direction. His eyes were also burnt and bloody. I looked around to see who he might mean and saw two people huddled together on the other side of the road, wearing some sort of religious garments. I went to them.

"Perhaps I can help you."

"What nonsense are you talking? There is no healing for this type of injury. As long as those followers of the false god exist, we will be outcasts in our own land. They alone bear the responsibility for our injuries. We can't be healed until they're sorry for the damage they've done, and I don't mean just pretending to be sorry. They have to be really sorry."

I stood up and stepped away, confused by the hatred that so consumed both groups that they would rather be wounded and in pain than give up their "rights" as martyrs. To my right, I heard a small sound. It almost sounded like a whimper, but I didn't see anyone, so I almost missed it until I heard it again. There was no mistaking it this time. I jumped into the ditch on the side of the road and found a young woman holding a baby to her chest. She looked in my direction with one eye and I could see that the other had a gash across it.

"Please," she said. "You said you have

medicine?"

My eyes filled with tears and my fingers fumbled with my bag. "Yes...yes, I do. Here, let me help you." I put the Balm of Gilead on her face and almost immediately, it began to heal. The redness and puffiness began to go down. She held out her baby and I could see that it was gray. I realized that her child had died, and she didn't know or wasn't ready to believe.

"Please help me," She said with hope and desperation in her face. My heart sank. I didn't have medicine for this. I had medicine for healing, not bringing back the dead. Suddenly, I felt a hand on my shoulder. I looked up. It was Him.

"This can be healed in My house," He said.

I turned to the young woman. "We have what your baby needs, but not here. You'll need to come with us through the Valley of the Shadow of Death to His house. It won't be easy, but He can heal your child there. Will you come?"

A sob tore from the depths of her chest. "You can heal her there? You're sure?"

"I'm sure," I said, not even looking at Him. I already knew that if He said He could heal it, He could heal it. He didn't need to impress anyone with claims He couldn't deliver.

I stood to help her out of the ditch. She

stumbled, but I held onto her. I could see that her leg was hurt by the way that she walked so we moved slowly. As we walked toward the Valley of the Shadow of Death, He turned to me and said, "You stay here and look for others who are willing to accept your help. I'll take her from here. I'll return when there are others who need help to My house."

"They won't accept my help."

"Many won't because they're more attached to being right than they are to being whole. They've turned being wounded into a badge of spirituality, not realizing that their woundedness is a memorial to their ego. They could be whole, but they'd have to give up their status as victims and they'd rather be victims. However, there are some who are tired of being hurt and just want it to stop, no matter what the cost. Help them and let the rest wallow in their martyrdom."

I must admit, it stung a little not to be allowed to return with Him, even though I understood why. The journey through the Valley of the Shadow of Death is one that must be made alone with Him, not with others. Even still, I felt rejected just a little as I turned back to the used-to-be-signpost.

Suddenly, I heard His voice from within me, so close and intimate. "How could I reject you? You're a part of Me...a part of Me that I trust to act on My behalf. You're the Me I've sent into this situation. Be Me here."

Doppelganger

There was only so much I could do here. I stood in the middle of the road, with my hands on my hips and looked around. Since the war had ended, travelers had started coming through this way again. I smiled at a couple as they passed me, whispering between themselves, so in love with each other that they couldn't notice anything else. A group of new believers gathered around the burnt signpost behind me, singing softly and leaving memorials for those they had lost. It was time for me to go.

I walked down the path to the Valley of the Shadow of Death and walked out onto the crossroads I had just left. I looked around, confused. Maybe I had gotten lost in the Valley. I turned back around and walked into the Valley of the Shadow of Death and out onto the crossroads I had just left. A thought flashed across my mind that He had rejected me, that He had closed the door and I wasn't allowed to return. Then I felt His hand on my shoulder. In relief, I hugged Him tightly.

He smiled and stepped back, opening an umbrella to cover us from the sprinkles that had started to fall. He waved at the other side of the road and I looked. There I was! I mean, I was there, and I was here. I was both places. I looked at Him. I was even more confused.

"This is the Valley of the Shadow of Death," He said. How many forms did this thing take? It was like going down the rabbit hole, the farther you went, the weirder it got.

"See yourself," He said and suddenly, we were beside the other me as she tried to help the sign worshipers from both sides. I saw frustration and disbelief on her face as they rejected her help in order to be offended with each other, choosing to be in pain by withholding forgiveness. Without warning, the scene stopped.

"Tell me why you wanted to come here after the war," He said.

"Well, after the war, I thought that there might be hurt people who needed help."

"Then why were you frustrated when these worshipers didn't want help? They obviously didn't believe they needed it."

"I see what You're saying. I did feel frustrated,

but mostly shocked. I could see that they were in pain, but they would rather be in pain and have a reason to hate the other side than be whole because it required them to let go. I didn't expect that. I thought that they would see that they needed help as easily as I could see that they needed help."

"What help do you think they needed?"

"Their eyes were damaged. They couldn't see. They had wounds and burns. The Balm of Gilead in my bag could have helped them."

"Are you sure?"

My time with Him had taught me that when He asked if I was sure, I probably shouldn't be.

"Why did the war start?" He asked.

"You said it was because of ego, because they hadn't made the journey through the Valley of the Shadow of Death."

"They started the war because they couldn't see Reality. All they could see was their own version of it. The wounds to their eyes were not caused by the war; they were the cause of the war. The Balm of Gilead wasn't made for this type of wound." He smiled at me with such love and affection that I could have lived a lifetime in that moment. In an instant, I realized that I loved Him, so much more than I ever thought I could love anyone.

"See yourself," He said and immediately, we

were beside the other me as she jumped into the ditch, searching for the source of the whimpering. I saw fear on her face, but not fear of harm. I saw fear born of genuine concern. I saw her find the woman and eagerly apply the Balm. Then I saw her face fall as the woman held out her dead baby. I almost cried with the other me. The scene stopped again.

"Why did you jump into that ditch?" He asked.

"I thought I heard a sound of pain and I just jumped. I don't know that there was a reason. I just reacted."

"You could have been hurt, you know. There could have been snakes in there or a bomb."

I paused. I hadn't considered that.

"You weren't thinking of yourself in that moment. You thought someone might be hurt and hidden. Your heart went out to whoever it was, and your body followed," He said. I nodded. He smiled again.

"See yourself," I saw the scene after He had left with the woman and her child. I saw myself return to the worshipers and, again, try to convince them to accept my help.

"Why did you want to come here after the war?"

"I'm not sure what you mean," I said.

"You said that you wanted to help those who

were wounded, yet after I left, you returned to the same people who didn't want your help. You didn't continue looking for the hidden wounded. You didn't help the other wounded you could see."

"I guess I thought that I could convince them to let me help them."

"You mean that you thought you could convince them to change." He looked at me like He could see everything. He saw into every corner and even the shadows were bright to Him. I smiled weakly.

"Yes. I guess I thought that if I could convince them to let me help them, they would stop being so angry with each other."

"You thought you could stop the war?"

"Maybe. I didn't realize it then, but maybe."

"When you leapt into the ditch to help a person you couldn't even see, you acted out of love. When you kept trying to help people who didn't want your help, you acted out of pride and the desire to change them, to control them. You weren't made to change people. You were made to love them. Do you see the difference?"

"I do. Trying to help people who didn't want my help wasn't wrong, but it did delay me in helping those who did want it and were ready to accept it."

"That's a good point," He said, nodding in

agreement. "The Valley of the Shadow of Death helps you to make better decisions, decisions not based on 'right or wrong' but on wisdom."

"By the way, what happened with the woman and her child?" I asked, turning toward Him.

"I took them to My house and healed her daughter. Both have spent the last few days healing and resting. I don't know if I've ever told you this, but I love children. I've spent the last few days rocking the baby to sleep and singing lullabies like a Paw-Paw. There's nothing quite so perfect as rocking a little one to sleep, with them nestled on your chest and their head under your chin."

I chuckled to myself at the image of Him with an expression of perfect bliss, falling asleep with a baby in His arms. I honestly didn't know who rocked whom to sleep. He closed the umbrella and turned toward His house.

"Are you ready to go?" He asked.

"I am," I said...and I was.

The Wall

The banging is what woke me. For a second, I thought I had a pounding headache, but quickly realized that it was just pounding, as in construction. I rolled over in my bed with a groan and then decided that there would be no more sleeping today. Huffing, I sat up and blew my hair out of my face.

I grabbed my bathrobe, put it on, and went into the front room where He was already sitting at the table, reading and drinking a cup of coffee.

"Good morning," He said brightly. I grumped in response and headed to the kitchen to pour myself a cup of coffee. I sat down across from Him and took a sip of "morning heaven."

"What's the pounding?" I asked as the caffeine started to work.

"Oh, they're building something down on the corner."

"Hmmmm. Maybe they're building a new

sign," I said optimistically. The look on His face said that would be interesting and unlikely.

"I don't know why they would rebuild a sign after going to such great lengths to destroy it," was all He said before returning to His book.

"What are you reading?" I asked, awake enough to be curious.

"Crossword," He said before getting up and going to the kitchen. "Do you want some bacon? How about some eggs? I'm making biscuits, or I could make my world-famous French toast."

"All of that sounds good," I said, suddenly starting to get hungry. "Do I have time to quickly shower and dress before it's ready?"

"Sure, go ahead," He said as He moved around the kitchen. I left my cup on the table and hurried to get ready.

After breakfast, the sounds of construction continued. I tried to work on a puzzle, but the noise kept distracting me. I looked out the front window, trying to catch a glimpse of what they were building, but, in the daylight, all I could see were trees and a general sense of movement. Finally, I could stand it no longer. I found Him in the garden.

"Would You mind if I went to see what they're building?"

"Not at all. It will be nice to have an

explanation for all of that pounding," He said as He tied Morning Glory vines to a trellis. They were in full bloom and the royal blue trumpets were exquisite.

As I neared the corner of His yard, I could see the reason for the construction. I stopped walking and just stood in shock. They were building a wall! They were building a wall to block off part of the path that the travelers took. I took a step or two closer. I could see a tall wall made of wood and stone with a small gate in the center and a big lock on this side. There was an opening in the gate through which whoever was on the other side could be seen. Either side of the wall was flush against the mountains so there was no way around it.

I turned and ran back to the garden, finding Him still there, tending His grapevines which were heavy with dark purple fruit. When I told Him about the wall, His eyebrow raised slightly but other than that, He gave no indication that it bothered Him, but it bothered me. If they built a wall, it would block people from seeking His house. The fact that it didn't seem to bother Him bothered me too. Truthfully, I was angry with Him for seeming not to care about those whose way would be blocked. It was like He had no sense of what this wall meant.

By the next day, the construction was complete. I sat across the table from Him, while He read His crossword, stewing about how He didn't seem to care about those people who were seeking Him but unable to get past the wall.

Without looking up, He said, "You're bothered." I semi-glared at Him. "Do you want to talk about it or would you prefer to just stare at Me? I'm ok with either."

I put my cup down harder than necessary. "I just don't think You understand what's at stake for these people," I said. "I thought You cared about them and I'm really surprised that it seems like You don't."

He put the book down and smiled at me. "Let's go take a look at it then," He said.

We went to the corner, past the forest. There was the wall, just as I'd seen earlier. There was a new guard shack near the gate where people took turns guarding the gate and challenging people who wanted to come through. We went to the current guard, a young man with short, brown hair and an air of intensity about him.

"What is the purpose of this wall?" He asked the young man.

"This wall is to protect us from evildoers who gather around other signs," he said.

"And how does it do that?"

"Well, I suppose I can tell you since you're on

this side. When someone wants to pass this way, we look through this window in the gate and ask them if they have been to any other signs apart from the one here. We ask if they believe there is any other sign other than the one here. If they answer 'yes' to either of those questions, they can't come in. The risk is just too great. Even if they say 'no' we make them tell us about the sign here, just to confirm that they've actually seen it. If they deviate in any way from what we've been taught, they can't come in. We have to keep the disruptive element out. Even if they look good and we let them in, we watch them really carefully until they've proven themselves trustworthy. It's about protecting the peace."

"I see," He said.

"It's a good system," the young man stated intently.

"Hmmmmmm," He replied as He led me away with His hand on my elbow.

After we got a little distance away, I whispered, "See what I mean?" He smiled. Sometimes, I hate that smile that tells me I'm missing something important, especially because it's always right.

"Ok. What am I missing? I can see it on Your face that I'm missing something."

"Look here," He said as He waved to the side

of the path back to His house. There was a ditch that ran through the middle of an especially thick bunch of trees. Down in that ditch, I saw the top of a mop of hair over two eyes that darted around.

"There's a person there!" I said, quietly.

"Yes. He's making a way around the wall."

"But...but...where did he come from?" I turned around, looking for some sort of path this young man could have taken.

"You were upset about the sign worshiper's attempts to control access to Me, to My house," He said. I nodded, my eyes wide, knowing He was about to reveal a great mystery to me.

"You forgot the deeper truth. You can't keep Love in any more than you can keep it out. Love finds a way. If there is no way, Love makes a way. No one comes to Me because of their thoughts or feelings. They come to Me because I called them. We're drawn to each other like magnets. The Love in that invitation finds a way to overcome obstacles, no matter what they are. There is no wilderness too wild or desert too deserted that Love will not transform it into a way to My house."

I watched as the man from the ditch climbed out and made a dash down the path I knew led to God's house. I looked farther up the mountain and saw another face, hiding behind a tree, and then another, farther up, crouched behind a boulder.

"I'm sorry," I said as my eyes filled with tears. "I forget who You are sometimes, not just that You're Him, but that You're Love."

He led me back to His house as tears streamed down my face. As we neared the door, He turned and took my face in His hands, wiping the tears away. "It is my great joy to remind you that I am Love because I am Love for you."

The Sign 2

I felt like my feet were on fire, like my skin was on too tight. I turned and repositioned myself, but it didn't do any good. The discomfort was in my heart, not my chair. After trying to concentrate on the book I was reading for a few more minutes, I set it aside with a sigh. My mind just couldn't stay still. I had to go find Him.

He was in the front yard, planting a cherry tree. I wouldn't have thought of Him as someone who enjoyed yard work, but the look of bliss and contentment on His face told me that I would have been wrong. He was completely at home with dirt smudged across His forehead.

"Can I help?" I asked even though He had the tree mostly planted.

"Of course," He said. "This young lady will need some water once I've finished putting her in her new home." I went to get the hose and turn on the water, not too strong but more than a trickle. He was finished by the time I got back.

"One day, she will stretch her branches across the sky and bear the brightest, sweetest cherries you could possibly imagine. Today, however, she needs us to take care of her and teach her how to grow into herself." He said, wiping His face and taking the hose from me.

"What have you named her?" I asked.

"Mora...Mora the Cherry Tree," He said with a smile over our shared joke that may or may not have actually been a joke. It was hard to tell with Him. His world was equal parts practical and whimsical.

My plan was to talk with Him about what was going on in my head but seeing Him there brought me into peace.

We walked into the house together. Since it was near lunchtime, I started to get things ready while He cleaned up. Almost immediately, my mind was elsewhere, and I was engulfed by that restless feeling again. I couldn't put it off anymore. I had to talk with Him about it.

During lunch, we chatted and talked about the day, but whereas before, I felt like I could talk about anything, today all I could think about was the one thing I didn't want to talk about. I realized He was sitting across the table in silence, just looking at me.

I thought that maybe He had said something, and I was supposed to respond, but didn't because I wasn't listening. Oh, my goodness, I wasn't listening, was I? Just great.

"You have something on your mind," He said. "Would you like to talk about it now or later?"

"I'm sorry. I guess my mind was elsewhere." I shifted in my seat. It felt like something was going to explode out of my chest if I didn't say something. "I've been thinking about the sign and the wall," I began, looking at the table.

"And…"

"And without the sign to guide them, people are lost. Yes, there are those who are finding a way around, but they were already looking for Your house. They knew that it existed even if they didn't know how to get here. What about those who don't know that there's something to be found?"

"Ah yes. There are those. Eventually, they will see the path and feel the call in their heart. Everyone does."

"And what about those who manage to get past the wall? That particular group of sign-worshipers seems so certain that they're right that I don't think they'll point people to Your house. They seem to want agree-ers rather than searchers."

He was silent, looking at me like He was

waiting for me to come to a realization that He already knew.

"I just feel like we should do something," I said, still hinting, scavenging around the edges of what I really wanted to say, almost afraid to say it because then it would be real.

"What do you think we should do?" He asked quietly.

"Well, I thought about building another sign, but I realized that they would just tear it down."

"Probably," He agreed.

"What if I went there and told people?" Now that I had started to get to the core of what was on my heart, it all rushed out. "What if I became the new sign?"

He let out a breath, like He'd been holding it in. He leaned forward and put His cup of coffee on the table.

"I've been waiting for you to talk with Me about this." He said. "Ever since we went to look at the wall, I could see how much the thought of people not being able to come to My house troubled you. The thought of them being lost and not knowing how to be found upset you. Finding that young woman and her baby changed something in your heart. In that moment, you found someone who mattered more to you than yourself." He paused for a breath and I rushed in.

"I've given it a lot of thought. You're right. Something happened to me when I found that young woman; it was like I found what I was made to do. In that moment, I didn't feel like me anymore. I felt like Love in motion. I don't want to do this because I think I'm supposed to. I want this to be what I'm supposed to do because I'm going to do it anyway." I sucked my breath in as it sank in what I'd said. I was horrified at my boldness and afraid of what He might say. I hoped He wouldn't think I was being disrespectful.

He chuckled softly, then louder, then began to laugh out loud until it shook the whole room. Tears filled my eyes.

"You are so beautiful," He said, "and you just have no idea." I didn't really know what to say to that, so I said nothing. "When did you want to go?"

"To be honest, I hadn't thought that far ahead. I was just afraid You wouldn't let me go, that You would tell me it was dangerous, and I should stay where it was safe."

"It is dangerous, but only in a different way than staying here is dangerous. I don't want to control you. You can't love someone and try to control them at the same time. Control destroys love and love destroys control. When you love someone, you love who they are, not who they would be if only they did what you said. Control is the love of self; it's a business arrangement. Control says 'I love you as long as you are what I want you to be. If you aren't what I want you to be, then I don't love you anymore.' That's not love; it's a business transaction. I love you, as you are, as you were, and as you will be."

"What happens now?" I asked, unsure of where to go from here.

"You can come and go as you wish," He said. "There may be times that I come to you because I long for your company. I hope that you'll come share dinner with me and the occasional walk in the garden."

My eyes became misty. "Of course."

"Do you remember how it was when you were at the crossroads after the war? The closeness and intimacy we felt even after I left to take the woman and her child to My home?" I nodded. I remembered.

"It will be like that unless, of course, you're here, and then it will be like this," He said with a smile. I saw no sorrow in His face. I half expected there to be since I was leaving His house. "You're leaving My house, but you're not leaving Me, and I will never leave you," He said as if He could read my thoughts.

"Thank you," I said.

"For what? For loving you? Believe me, it wasn't that hard," He replied, laughing.

Sleeping that night was like a weight had been lifted off my shoulders. It was the sweetest sleep I had ever had. The next morning, I woke early, ate breakfast, got dressed, and packed a bag. He walked me to the crossroads. I hugged Him. He held me for a moment and pulled away slightly, looking me in the face.

"There are two things to remember. First, My house is right around the corner and you're welcome, no matter day or night. I am a part of you and you are a part of Me. We cannot be separated from each other. Second, there are many counterfeits, but true love pours itself out into others. It holds nothing back because love isn't about worthiness; it's not about anything. It simply is. You will pour yourself out for others and some will respond like Mora the Cherry Tree and blossom, and some will reject you. That shouldn't change who you are. Be Love because that's who you are; that's who we are together. Love the people, whether they change or not and know that, no matter what happens, I love you."

I nodded. He let go of me and stepped back. I smiled, turned, and walked over to the platform where the sign had once stood. I stepped on top of it and raised my arm, my hand pointing down the path to God's house. He smiled at me one last time before turning around and walking down the path where I was pointing. The travelers passed around me, some looking at me strangely.

Several hours passed with me standing and pointing, or sometimes just standing when my arm got tired, before someone asked why I was standing on that podium. I smiled broadly and said, "This is the way to God's house."

"Really?!" They said. "We've been looking for the path, but the men at the gate told us that it had been lost. Tell us about it." And so, I did.

Home

The night was cold as I sat on the platform where, so long ago, that original sign had been. It was the only time of the day when I had quiet. It had been many years since I first stepped onto the platform to act as the new sign and even more years since I had first come seeking God's house. My eyelids felt so heavy and my head sank slowly to my chest. Suddenly, the atmosphere changed, and I was wide awake. I looked around and saw Him standing at the crossroads. I jumped to my feet and ran to Him, without even thinking. He smiled and opened His arms to me. It was the first time I remembered Him doing that. I ran into His embrace.

"It's so good to see you, my dear friend," I said. "Where are we going today? Is it another trip through the Valley of the Shadow of Death?"

He smiled broadly. "It's time for you to come home."

"Home? What do you mean? Right now? I mean I can leave for a little while. I feel like we're making some progress here. More people have been coming through asking questions and there have been a lot of great discussions lately. In fact, one of the travelers has been following me everywhere. I feel like she's almost ready to make the journey herself."

"Where is she now?" He asked. I turned around to point her out and stopped short.

"Ooohhhhhhhh," I breathed. I saw my body still on the platform where the sign had stood so long ago. With my chin resting on my chest, it almost looked like I was asleep. My eyes filled with tears. "I thought it would hurt more. I have always heard that there are regrets, that your life flashes before your eyes. But this didn't hurt at all. Are you sure it's true? I mean, am I really...?"

He smiled at me patiently. "When you live a life of dying to yourself, the final journey is easy. The only difference is that this time you won't return to your body, but you were never your body. Most people never understand that truly living depends on truly dying."

"But I still had so much to do," I said, with a tinge of longing. He put His arm around my shoulders.

"Those are for someone else to complete. It

was given to you to build a new foundation upon which others would continue to build. You've done your part and now it's time to let them do theirs. Life is not an event; it's a continuum. For you, it's time to come home. For them, it's time to awaken." I nodded in agreement and understanding. "Besides," He continued, "it looks like you've already passed your mantle on to someone." He nodded in the direction where my body sat. Beside the platform, the small shape of a young woman lay sleeping, covered in my long, wool coat. My eyes filled with tears again.

"She's the one I was telling you about. Just showed up one day and never left. She started following me around, then eating every meal with me, then decided she wanted to fix the meals for me...and asking a million questions. She went through a lot to get here and I'm happy to have known her. I think You're going to like her when she decides to take the path to Your house."

"I already do. And don't worry about this young one," He said, turning back toward His house and stepping down the path, "She'll make the journey to My house before the sun sets today." He reached His hand out to me. "Are you ready to go home?"

"I am," I said as I took His hand and laced my fingers with His.

"Then let's go home," He said, and we did.

There is Only Love

I am in love with Love.

I love You

And have become Love,

With You, beside You, and in You.

I have become

Both the Lover and the Beloved,

Alternately and simultaneously.

We are One.

There is no beginning.

There is no end.

There is only Us

And We are Love.

There is only Love.

www.ingramcontent.com/pod-product-compliance
Lightning Source LLC
Chambersburg PA
CBHW072043170626
46811CB00008B/3140